# Whale of a Tale

**story by Barbara Pearl**
**illustrated by Cathy Janson**

**Crane Books**

To contact Project F.O.L.D.
Folding with Origami for Learning and Development
for information on other Crane Books, products, and workshops,
call or write: 668 Stony Hill Road, #233
Yardley, PA  19067
(215) 321-5556
Email: info@mathinmotion.com

Visit us at www.mathinmotion.com

Production layout - Robert Grau
Cover graphic design - Jeanine Testa
Reading Consultants - Phyllis Betz, Ph.D., Mary Robertson, Ph.D.
The illustrations for this book were created in acrylics and pen and ink with Winsor and Newton paints
on Aquarelle Arches water color paper. The typeface is Dom Casual.

Ages 3-8, Grades: Pre-K-2

Summary: A magic square transforms into different shapes unfolding new adventures until finally
it joins a family of penguins. Features learning activities and instructions on how to fold a whale.
1. Imagination-Fiction  2. Storytelling-Fiction  3. Animals  4. Origami  5. Shapes

Other books by Barbara Pearl: *Math in Motion: Origami in the Classroom K-8*
Available in Spanish: *Matemáticas en Movimiento: Origami en el Salón de Clases K-8*

A percentage of sales is donated to humanitarian organizations.

*Special thanks to our mother, Helene Selig and F. G. J.*

ISBN: 0-9647924-7-8

10 9 8 7 6 5 4 3 2 1

First Edition

In loving memory of Jason Seth Houten
LOVE YOU FOREVER

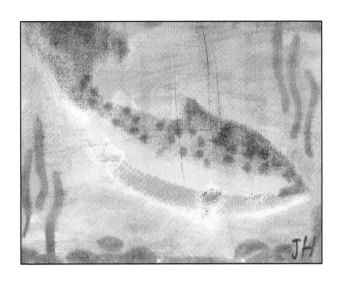

Once there
was a magic
square

that turned into a kite

along rivers

and valleys,

above mountains

and hills,

until
one day
it
crashed
into
a tree.

# With a big splash, it fell into the sea

where there were baby turtles and manatees.

# So it turned into a whale.

Is that a fishy tale?

The whale swam all around,

up
jumping over the waves,

and diving d o w n to eat.

# Then the whale saw baby seals and birds playing.

head
her
on
stood
mammal
clever
very
this
So

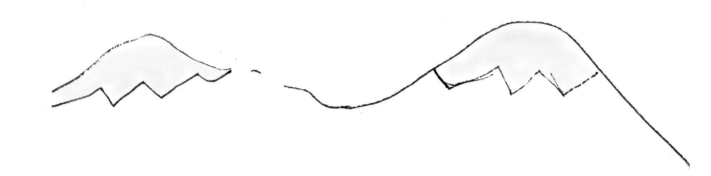

**and became
        a penguin instead.**

# How to Fold a Whale

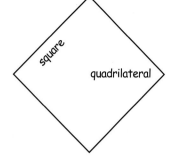

**1** Start with a 6 to 8 inch square sheet of paper on the table so it looks like a diamond. *(See How to Fold a Square from a Rectangle.)*

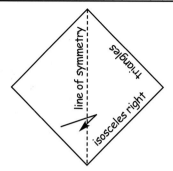

**2** Fold the right point over to meet the left point (fold in half). Unfold. Find the center crease (line of symmetry).

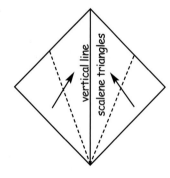

**3** Fold the lower right and left sides to meet at the center crease (line of symmetry).

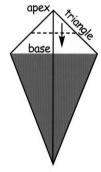

**4** It looks like a kite. Now fold the apex (top point) down to the base line to form a small triangle.

## *How to Fold a Square from a Rectangle

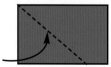   

Materials: Recycle gift wrap, magazine covers, or flyers. Traditional origami paper is available at arts and crafts stores or online at www.mathinmotion.com